MONKEY

A TRICKSTER TALE FROM INDIA

Gerald McDermott

Harcourt Children's Books
Houghton Mifflin Harcourt
Boston   New York   2011

Harcourt Children's Books is an imprint of
Houghton Mifflin Harcourt Publishing Company.
www.hmhbooks.com

The illustrations in this book were created with textured papers
hand-colored by the artist with fabric paint and ink, then mounted
on heavy watercolor paper.
The text type was set in Goudy Sans Bold.
The display lettering was created by Gerald McDermott.
Designed by Gerald McDermott and Judythe Sieck

Library of Congress Cataloging-in-Publication Data
McDermott, Gerald.
Monkey : a trickster tale from India / by Gerald McDermott.
p. cm.
Summary: Crocodile wants to feast on Monkey's heart and Monkey
must outsmart him if he is to enjoy eating mangoes all day.
ISBN 978-0-15-216596-3
[1. Folklore—India.] I. Title.
PZ8.1.M159Mon 2010
398.2—dc22
[E]
2009007977

Manufactured in China
LEO 10 9 8 7 6 5 4 3 2 1
4500271904

The tale of clever Monkey and dull-witted Crocodile is
from the Buddhist tradition. The story is part of an ancient
collection of folklore, fables, and legends called the Jataka
tales, which originated in India in the third and fourth
centuries B.C. and circulated throughout Southeast Asia
for thousands of years. Translated from the original
Sanskrit into English in the nineteenth century, most
notably by W. H. D. Rouse in his 1895 work for the
University of Cambridge Press, the 547 stories have since
been published in countless editions in many languages.

For this final volume in my series of six trickster tales,
I was inspired to tell this popular story—known as the
Sumsumara-Jataka—because of its wonderful mixture of
morality and irony. It is Monkey who has the "heart"
that Crocodile lacks, and brute force cannot prevail. The
playfulness of the story lent itself to a bold collage of cut
and torn papers, some from India and Southeast Asia.
The floral design on the cover, commonly referred to in
the West as paisley, is known throughout India as the
"raw mango" motif and is the basis for a key element
in my telling.

I'm grateful to Sujata Shahane for her valuable suggestions
and to her remarkable daughters, Rhea and Tanvi, for
their enthusiastic support. My gratitude, as well, goes to
book artist Tania Baban-Natal for sharing the technique of
teasing apart moistened handmade paper to create a furry
edge. Finally, deep thanks to my editor, Jeannette Larson,
paragon of perceptiveness and patience.

—G.M.

For Mallory, Hannah, and Tanner

Monkey!

Chattering Monkey.
He lived high in a tree on the banks
of the wide, flowing river.

Monkey jumped so high and so fast through the treetops, no one could catch him. But catching Monkey was exactly what Crocodile wanted to do.

"Mmmmm," murmured hungry Crocodile. "How delicious a monkey heart would be!"

Crocodile slithered into the water.
"Good morning, Monkey!" he called out.

"Good morning, Crocodile!" answered Monkey.
"Where are you going?"

"To the island in the middle of the river,"
answered Crocodile.

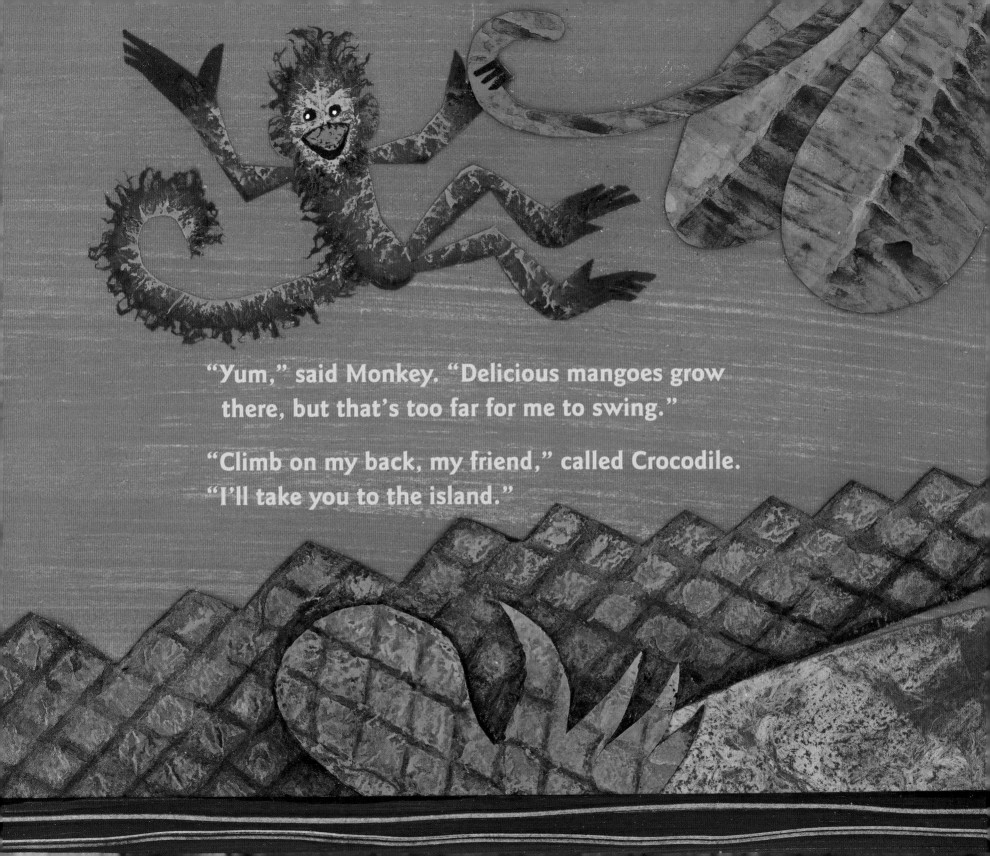

"Yum," said Monkey. "Delicious mangoes grow there, but that's too far for me to swing."

"Climb on my back, my friend," called Crocodile. "I'll take you to the island."

Monkey swung down from the tree
and hopped onto Crocodile's scaly back.

As Crocodile glided through the deep,
dark water, he sank lower and lower.

Monkey began to get wet.

"Oh, my goodness—I cannot swim!" shouted Monkey.

"How well I know," said Crocodile. "Now I'm going to eat your heart!"

"Eat my heart?" said Monkey. "What a pity. I left it up in the tree!"

"You left your heart in the tree?" Crocodile grumbled. "What a nuisance."

Crocodile returned with Monkey
to the muddy brown riverbank.
As soon as they reached the
shore, Monkey leaped off
Crocodile's back and scampered
up a tall tree, laughing
and chattering.

"Look, my heart is here!"
called Monkey from the treetop.
"Just climb up and get it!"

Crocodile grunted and thrashed
and swam away.

Now Monkey wanted the delicious mangoes more than ever. He leaped from treetop to treetop until he discovered some large rocks far downriver.

He saw that if he skipped across the rocks to the island, he could feast on mangoes every day.

The next morning, Crocodile came swimming down the river, looking for Monkey.

He heard Monkey chattering. He saw Monkey jump from tree to rock to island.

"I shall pretend I'm a rock," said Crocodile.
"When Monkey jumps on me, I will snap him up,
heart and all!"

Crocodile lay low in the water all day long.

When Monkey had eaten his fill, he headed for home with all the mangoes he could carry. He jumped off the island onto a rock in the river. He was about to jump onto another rock, but something was wrong.

Monkey looked closer, then called out in a cheery voice, "Hello, Rock!"

Crocodile was silent. He lay low in the water.

Monkey called out again. "I say, good evening, Rock!"

Crocodile said nothing.

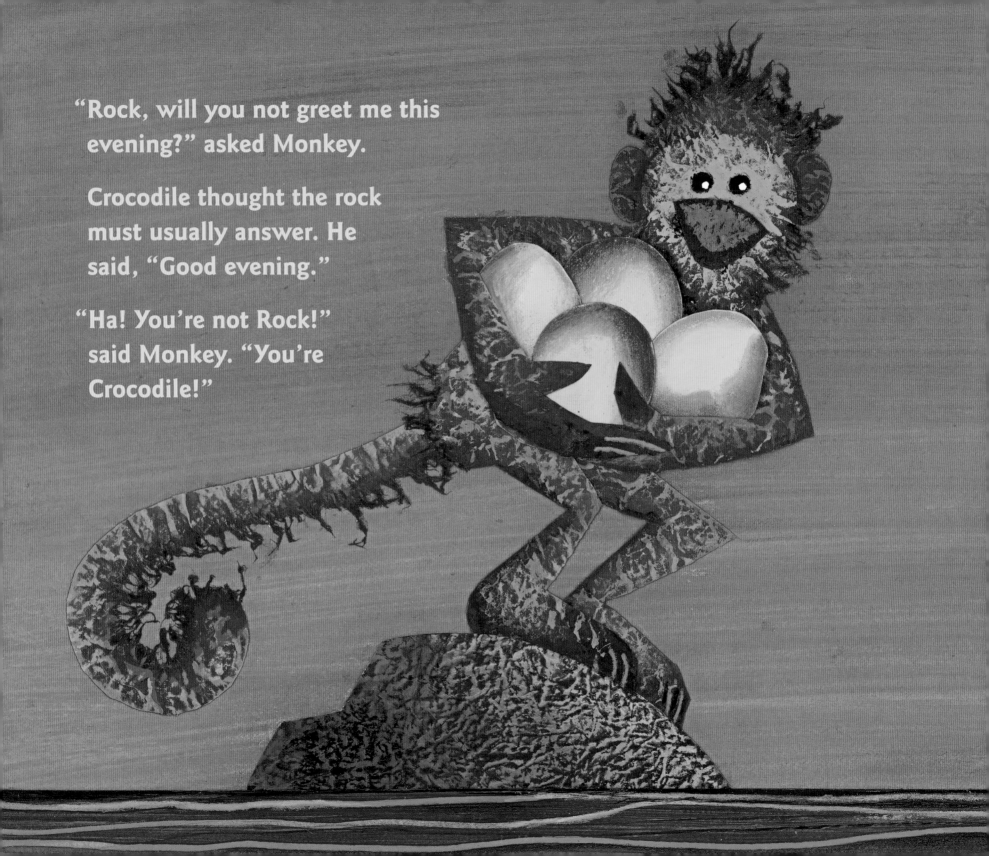

"Rock, will you not greet me this evening?" asked Monkey.

Crocodile thought the rock must usually answer. He said, "Good evening."

"Ha! You're not Rock!" said Monkey. "You're Crocodile!"

"I'm as good as a rock," said Crocodile. "You can jump on me to get to the other side."

"Oh, what a splendid idea!" said Monkey. "Here I come!"

Monkey got ready to leap. Crocodile closed his eyes and opened his jaws.

But instead of leaping, Monkey popped
a mango right into Crocodile's mouth.

Bang! Crocodile snapped his jaws shut.

Quickly, Monkey jumped on Crocodile's nose,
then onto the muddy brown riverbank.

Laughing and chattering, Monkey scampered
up a tree and swung from branch to branch.

"Your teeth may be sharp,"
Monkey shouted to Crocodile.
"But your mind is dull!"

Now Monkey feasts on
delicious mangoes every day.

Crocodile lies low in the
water, keeping an eye on him.

And when Monkey crosses
the river to go home,
he is always careful
to jump on a rock,
not on a crocodile.